Pictures and poe   **ır**
is just so good th

MW00929203

..., -ᵖ---᷍---᷍---, rᵀ0
Football Hall of Fame

I'm so happy to see a book that relates to kids and also conveys the message to parents that baseball is still just a game.
— **Jay Johnstone**, former 20-year
major leaguer and co-founder of
Sporthings

An endearing collection of poems that puts you right back in the action; through a child's perspective you will get inside the game of baseball and to the real heart of sports! These poems will provide you with wonderful insights into the bigger game of life that will put a smile on your face and a lump in your throat. From the first day of practice jitters to Grandma watching a game, you will remember what it's like to hear, "Going, Going, Gone!" This is a must-have treasure for every baseball fan!
— **Jeaney Garcia**, Los Angeles
coordinator, Positive Coaching
Alliance

Hey Batter Batter *captures the essence of the joy—and the frustrations—of kids' baseball in image and rhyme. I thoroughly enjoyed this collection. I can't wait to give a copy to my son.*
— **John Dewan,** owner,
Baseball Info Solutions

After forty-five years of coaching I thought I heard it all—but it was great to hear it again!
— **Gene Manley,** youth
baseball coach

Shane's ode to the game is both fun and reflective, moments and memories every boy (and every former boy) will identify with. Whether it is Dad coaching from the sidelines, the right fielder who might be useful as the math exam approaches, or deciding how hard to run when the ball is hit, these glimpses of the action bring it all back.

Shane puts us out on the field of our dreams, remembers the snacks and rally caps, and gives us images to treasure and remember.

— **Richard K. Moore,** librarian,
Orange County Department
of Education

Bill Shane is a champion of fair play and sportsmanship. In **Hey Batter Batter** *he has captured the meaning and joy of youth sports. By stressing the "fun" aspects of baseball, he reminds us that we shouldn't take the game—or ourselves—too seriously. I give this book a perfect 10!*

— **Peter Vidmar,** Olympic
gymnastics champion, author
of *Risk, Originality, and Virtuosity,
the Keys to a Perfect 10*

Hey Batter Batter *captures all that is magical about Little League baseball. In fact, it refreshes my memory as to why I named my only son Tanner, after the shortstop of the Bad News Bears and bought him his first mitt when he was only seven days old. Thanks for the memories Bill!*

— **Dave Smith,** sports agent and
author of *From the Prom to the
Pros*

Hey
Batter
Batter

Hey Batter Batter

A COLLECTION OF BASEBALL POEMS FOR KIDS

KIDS SPORTS PRESS

An imprint of

SEVEN LOCKS PRESS

Santa Ana, California

Seven Locks Press
P.O. Box 25689
Santa Ana, CA 92799
(800) 354-5348

Individual Sales. This book is available through most bookstores or can be ordered directly from Seven Locks Press at the address above.

Quantity Sales. Special discounts are available on quantity purchases by corporations, associations, and others. For details, contact the "Special Sales Department" at the publisher's address above.

Printed in the United States of America

Library of Congress Cataloging-in-Publication Data
is available from the publisher
ISBN 1-931643-20-2

Photos courtesy of © R. Symanski

Cover and Interior Design by Heather Buchman, Costa Mesa, CA

I would like to dedicate this book to the thousands of volunteer managers, coaches, umpires, scorekeepers and all others who help to make baseball such an incredibly rewarding experience for millions of kids around the world.

And, of course, I want to thank the kids who actually play the game for being a constant reminder to the adults that no matter how important championships, tournaments and All-Stars seem to be, it really, really REALLY is just a game . . .

Hey Batter Batter

Where else can you go
Where silly talk is good?

In fact, the coaches say
This is something that you should.

"Humbabe, humbabe, humbabe!"
"Hey batter, batter, batter!"

They tell us that it's good
To do this kind of baseball chatter.

Imagine if they wanted us
To do this talk in school.

"Hey teacher, teacher, teacher!"
You know, I think that's pretty cool!

Sliding

Moms don't really understand
Why ballplayers have to slide.

They think we'll get hurt and way too dirty
But I'll bet they've never even tried.

Sliding's so great, you skid on the ground.
And you stop right on top of the base.

Of course you get dirty, that's part of the fun!
The dirtier the better in this case!

I'll bet that if moms (and dads) would go out
And tumbled and rolled around and slid.

They'd have a lot more fun—like they probably did
Back when they were a kid!

Chill Out, Dad!

My coach says to choke up more.
My dad yells out I'm fine.
Coach says use a 28 bat.
Dad shouts 29.

Which one do I listen to?
What's a boy to do?
I am only ten years old
And they're both forty-two.

Someone will get angry
And I'm stuck in the middle.
How do you think that I can solve
This very difficult riddle?

I know! I know! I've got it!
Can this really work?
I hope that neither one of them
Will think that I'm a jerk.

Somehow I will get the coach
To tell my dad the facts.
That there's really only just one coach.
And Dad, will you relax!

Just watch the game and laugh a lot.
Cheer—don't shout advice.
Maybe you'll find that watching games
Can actually be nice!

88 Keys to Success

One of the kids on our team
I found out.
Would rather play piano than ball!

He's one of the weakest players on our team.
Why is he playing at all?

Go play your Beethoven or whatever you do!
Why are you doing this too?

We'd be a much better team—and win lots more games.
If we didn't get stuck with you.

I shouldn't be like this.
I know that it's mean.
I know it's a little bit cruel.

He's a really nice guy.
And everyone knows
He's one of the smartest at school.

Maybe it helps him to do something new.
Something where he's not the best.

Maybe I'll help him to play a bit better.
And he'll help me with Friday's math test!

Around the Horn

After an out with no one on base
We throw the ball around.

All the infielders catch and throw
Then we return it to the mound.

I don't know where all of this started
Where this silly habit was born.

But I still think it's great when we whip that ball
All around the horn.

Talking Baseball

Baseball has a language
Just like a secret code.

Some of it is really new
Some over 100 years old.

Everyone knows what a shutout is
And of course a double play.

But what about an RBI?
Or a pitcher's ERA?

Give 'em the heat. Throw him the deuce.
Are you familiar with these?

What about a sacrifice fly?
Or lay down a suicide squeeze?

The list can just go on and on
But it's very clear to me

If you want to be a friend of mine
Know all about 6-4-3.

Catcher

This is sort of like Halloween.
I get to put on all this stuff.

The shin guards are great—now you can't see my legs
I feel like, real rough and tough.

The chest protector is like a big vest
Sort of like supercops wear.

And no matter how hard the ball might come in
I know that you can't hurt me there.

Of course, I'm only eight years old
And I need help getting it on.

And some of the things are, well, way too big.
But I'm almost, finally, done.

My favorite of all, of course, is the mask.
I put it on last like a pro.

I'm ready to play! On with the game!
Play Ball! I'm ready to go!

Oh, one more thing. I don't think I said.
And you might think I'm making it up.

But in order to catch they also make me wear
This, weird, funny thing called a cup!

Dark

My buddies and I were
Playin' ball at the park.

When Mom said "Time to come in!
It's really getting too dark!"

Too dark? She must be kidding!
Our game will soon be done.

It may not be as bright as day.
But please don't spoil our fun.

We're very nearly finished.
Who'll be the home run king?

But everyone knows that "way too dark"
Is one of those weird Mom things.

First Day of Practice

It's the first day of practice.
Who's on my team?

And far more important—
Is my coach going to scream?

Is he one of those guys
Who just wants to win?

Or will it be a fun team
That I'm on again?

The last two years
Were really lots of fun

And our coach was cool
Whether we lost or won.

But I've heard and I've seen
Plenty of those other guys

Where as long as you win
It doesn't matter if you're nice.

Well, I'll know real soon
Which type coach he's gonna be.

And whether the next three months
Will be fun or not for me.

School 1, Baseball 0

I have a big game today after school.
The winner will take over first.

School is so dull. I'm stuck here in class.
I can't imagine anything worse.

It's just 10 o'clock. Still five more hours.
I can only think of the game.

I'll never last! Go faster, clock!
Are the other kids thinking the same?

The Car Ride Home

Dad is driving us
Home from the game.

I'm tired, I'm hungry
He's probably the same.

On that grounder to you
Back in the third inning.

He asks what happened
"Start at the beginning."

I don't want to talk
About a game that is past

Whether my team is in
First place or last.

Just tell me that I
Had a wonderful game.

YOU might like talking about it
But I'm not the same.

Let's talk about something
ANYTHING else.

Or go have a hamburger
And time to ourselves.

Tossed

There's an idiot kid on the other team
Who likes to fool around.

And everyone knows he swears the most
Of anyone on the playground.

We played his team in a game today
You'll never guess what he did.

Yep, the umpire kicked him out of the game.
Not the manager or coach, but the kid.

He was called out at third on a very close play
He could either have been safe or out.

But he yelled at the ump some words I won't use
So the umpire kicked him out.

He won't be allowed to play the next game.
Parents talk about the message it sends.

But take it from me it also caused him
To lose all of his teammates as friends.

Snack Bar

Talk all you want.
Say what you must say.

About who's in first place
Or the Plays of the Day.

But most important to me is that
Before we leave in the car

To go home from the field . . .
We hit the Snack Bar!

The Injury

I don't know how it happened
But it hurts me when I throw.

Right there on my elbow
And just a bit below.

The doctor said to rest it.
Don't pitch, don't bat, don't play.

If you treat it right.
You'll be okay, two weeks from today.

Two whole weeks! There's just no way!
My team is gonna lose!

We'll no longer be in first place!
This is terrible, terrible news.

I told the coach to pitch me.
But just an inning or two.

He looked me right straight in the eye
And told me what he'd do.

He said "You're crazy! Just plain dumb!
There's not a chance in heaven.

Don't you want to play next year.
At the ripe old age of eleven?"

Watching On TV
With Dad

Sometimes when my dad comes home
He'll go straight and turn on the TV.

And turn on his favorite baseball game.
And say, "Come, Son, and watch it with me!"

I don't want to say that
I don't think it's great.
That I don't want to watch any more.

But the truth is that I love to be playing the game.
But watching on TV's a bore!

Keeping Score

Did you ever see the scorebook
Where they keep the official score?

Trying to figure out what it means
Is for me an impossible chore.

Sometimes it says 6–3
And sometimes a backwards K.

I don't get it. Who really cares?
We just want to play.

Dreamin'

I feel like Sammy Sosa.
Barry Bonds or Mark McGwire.

I'm staring down the pitcher.
Waiting for him to fire.

A big huge swing and there it goes!
Sailing over the wall.

It's time to show my home run trot.
It's time to "touch 'em all."

Well, sure I'm only six years old
And hitting off a tee.

But that's what I'll do when I'm a pro.
Just you wait and see.

New Player

Hey Tommy! Hey Billy!
Mary's on our team!
She gonna try to play with the boys!

Who is she kidding?
Why doesn't she go back
To Barbie and other girl toys?

Can she hit? Well, yeah
She's the best on the team.

Can she pitch?
Yeah, she's best in the school.

Hey Tommy! Hey Billy!
I thought we were friends!
Why are you calling me a fool?

My First Homerun

I remember my very first homerun
I got it while playing T-Ball.

I smashed the ball all the way to the pitcher.
We were both about 3 feet tall.

I took off for first while he bobbled the ball.
His throw, of course, wasn't caught.

I rounded the bag, and headed for second
Would I ever stop? I would not!

The next throw wound up in centerfield.
Like a rocket I took off for third.

The ball just kept rolling all the way to the fence.
While the centerfielder was watching a bird.

The coach said "Go! Go!" and I headed for home.
The fans were all shouting my name.

I slid into home, "Safe!" yelled the ump.
A homer in my very first game.

Now my big brother said
It was really on errors,
And wasn't a homerun at all.

But my mom and my dad
Said it WAS a homerun.
I really love playing baseball.

Temptation

The batter's box is gorgeous.
The baselines perfectly straight.

But let me tell you something
Every kid think's really great.

Run your feet right through those lines.
Make a royal mess!

Kick that chalk a million miles
From the east coast to the west.

The Man

At a major league game
And this may seem weird
There's one special guy that I love.

No, not one of the players
Or even a coach.
That's not who I'm thinking of.

It's the guy selling peanuts
With that incredible voice
Yelling at the top of his lungs.

"Peanuts! Get your peanuts!
Get peanuts here!"
The words just roll off his tongue.

Who can resist? You just have to buy!
I can hardly wait to get mine.

My dad says, "Two, please."
And now here they are.
It's peanut eatin' time.

Those Three
Magic Words

When I listen to a game on the radio
Three little words make my smile come on.

When a guy on my team hits a long fly ball
And the announcer says, "Going, going GONE!"

The Reward

The ball game is over
Well, that's what we thought.
The last pitch was thrown
And the last ball was caught.

But the parents were yelling
He was safe! He was out!
And we sure didn't know
What the fight was about.

Billy turned to me
And asked if we won.
I said, "Yeah, I think so."
But who cares? The game's done.

Now we can talk about
What really matters . . .
And it's not about runs
Or errors or batters.

I'm only seven, and Billy is eight.
And here, my friends, is the cold fact:
What we really, really want to know is . . .
What are we having for snack?

7th Inning Stretch

Want to know what's even more fun
Than making a spectacular catch?

Then go to a Major League Baseball game
And wait for the 7th inning stretch.

Out of your seat. Everyone up!
It's time to sing our song.

Take Me Out To The Ballgame.
And everyone sings along.

Bad Call

I led off the game and
Hit a grounder to third.
I ran like a rocket.
Then something weird occurred.

I got to first base
Beat the throw—there's no doubt.
But then I heard the umpire's
Voice scream, "You're out!"

I couldn't believe it!
He's wrong! That's not fair!
I jumped up and down
Threw my arms in the air.

I wanted to argue.
What could I do?
My manager said,
"I want to talk to you."

Oh, great, I thought.
He'll tell me to chill.
That yes, the ump blew it.
But sometimes everyone will.

Be a good sport
And all those words

That coaches must say
That sound really absurd.

But that's not what happened
He looked into my eyes
And told me something
That was quite a surprise.

He said, Dan, you are wrong.
You were definitely out.
Everyone knows it
Except you—you were out!

Like the NBA player
Who can't believe that he fouls.
And turns to the referee and
Yells, screams and howls.

We could see it from here
A lot better than you.
The ump got it right.
Now here's what to do.

Remember the story of the
Player (unnamed)
Who after strike three
Turned to the ump and complained.

The ump said you think that
I'm wrong and you're right?
Then look it up in the sports section
Of your paper tonight!

Foul Ball

When I go to a major league baseball game
I *always* take my glove.

You know what I want! What every kid wants!
It's the foul ball that we all dream of.

You just never know when it might happen.
When right at you it'll be hit.

So you've gotta be ready. Watch every pitch!
And be sure to have on your mitt.

Now that can be tricky, when eating a dog.
Eat—take a bite—glove . . . which?

There's really no choice. You've GOT to be ready.
Each and every pitch.

Imagine if they finally hit it to you
What would you tell them at school?
I had a chance, but I was drinking my coke.
That's impossible! How totally uncool!

Foul Ball II

There's something cool about Little League
That very few people know.

Something all kids think is great
And parent just say, "Oh, No!"

It has to do with foul balls
That go over the fence or the screen.

And head straight for the parking lot.
Yeah, you know what I mean.

A foul ball that's hit just right
Will land right on top of the hood.

And make a sound that makes parents jump
But the kids just say, "That was good!"

And every now and then
You'll hear the sound of broken glass.

And all the kids will sure agree.
They've never seen grown-ups run so fast!

Foul Ball III

I did it! I did it!
I just caught a foul ball!

I'll take it to school.
I'm feeling ten feet tall!

The ball landed a little bit off to my right.
I scrambled around on the ground.

I held it high for all to see!
I'm the luckiest kid around!

Late

There's one little thing that really bugs me.
It's something that I really hate.

My little brother and sister messing around.
Which means that I'm going to be late.

Is that fair? I'm ready to go.
After all, it is MY game.

And when I show up late
The coach will be mad.
And won't care when I say THEY'RE to blame.

Leading Off Base

I got a walk
Now I'm on first base
Listening to my coach's advice.

Go on the ground
Halfway on a fly
It all sounds so easy and nice.

But what if it's neither
A grounder or fly
But sort of halfway in-between?

What do I do?
Do I stay here or run?
Do you think that you know what I mean?

If it gets by the catcher
Then hustle to second.
Run hard like you're in a big race.

But what if it goes just
A little way off.
Do I go or stay here on the base?

If I do the wrong thing
The coach will be mad
And the players will treat me like dirt.
It's supposed to be fun

But why do I always
Worry about feeling so hurt?

New Hat

Some think that a baseball cap
Is really just something to wear.

But real players know that
It's important HOW you put on what's up there.

You've got to bend the bill a bit
Put a ridge just right in the top.

Pull it down over your eyes.
That's it . . . now more . . . now stop!

If you wear the hat just right.
I really think it's true.

That you'll feel like a real player.
And it'll help you play like one, too.

Tryouts

Today is the day
For my Little League tryout
I know I'm supposed to stay cool.

But what if I stink?
What will they think?
They'll laugh at me Monday at school.

It's been four long months
Since I've swung a bat
And six since I've played in a game.

And some of those kids
You know how they play . . .
They should be in the Hall of Fame!

They say don't worry
Just do your best.
But I'm the one on the spot.

It's supposed to be fun
Am I the only one
Who thinks that it's definitely not?

Who's idea is this?
Who is the genius?
Does he know that I'm sweating this out?
Is this good for the kids

Or what's good for the grownups?
Who is this really all about?

Photo Day

Well, today is the famous Photo Day.
When we have our pictures shot.

I suppose it's great for the parents.
But for the kids it's not so hot.

We stand in line and wait a lot
For it to finally be our turn.

The guy cracks some joke—we think it's dumb
Don't photographers ever learn?

But the worst part of all
Is that we're supposed to behave
Don't play, look ahead, and don't run.

Some mom says "Don't talk
And keep the line straight."
She might just as well say "No fun!"

But we're kids, we DO play.
And we throw, slide and catch.
Come on, do you know what I mean?

It's kind of weird, to be out with the kids
In uniform—and told to keep clean!

Statistics

It's the manager's wife
Who officially keeps score
And keeps track of hits, runs and errors.

But nobody really
Follows it closely.
In fact, hardly anyone cares.

But the manager knows.
Yes, the manager knows.
As if all of this really matters.

But I guess that he thinks
He's a professional manager.
Getting matchups for pitchers and batters.

He's sort of like Santa
Because he knows
If your season's been good or been bad.

He knows how often
Each player struck out.
And how many hits each one of us had.

The kids, of course,
Could also keep score

And tell if HE'S naughty or nice.
And sit him down,
Or tell him what's wrong
So HE won't make the same mistake twice.

Tears

I know I'm not supposed to cry
Out on the baseball field.

But sometimes I can't help it
Let me tell you how I feel.

Sometimes it's from losing . . .
I know I can't always win.

But I can't just go say "Good game"
And do it with a grin.

Sometimes it's because I made
An error or struck out.

Maybe when I'm older then
It won't make me go pout.

But the one that really ticks me off
Is when something is unfair.

Like an umpire calling me out at the plate
When I knew I slid in there.

My folks say that it's just a game
I'm out there to have fun.

Didn't they ever cry as kids?
Is it something they've never done?

The Playoffs are Coming

If you want to know
When the playoffs are coming
I'll tell you what to look for.

You can tell real easy
By watching the managers
As they start to yell and scream more.

I guess it's important
To them to finish first
They tell us that that's why we're here.

But I always thought
We were here to have fun
But the coaches get weirder each year.

They yell at the umpires
Over safe, out, fair, foul.
They yell whenever there's an error.

They yell if we're losing
They yell at each other
Maybe they should look in the mirror.

Or maybe we should simply
Let the kids take over.
Yeah—let's get rid of them all.

No parents. No coaches.
No screaming, no fighting.
Just let the kids go and play ball.

New Uniforms

They handed out the uniforms
At the team practice yesterday.

Pants and shirts and socks and belts.
It all looks A-OK!

We'll look just like the real Yankees.
Pinstripes and all!

I can't wait to put 'em on
And get out there and play ball.

There's just one tiny little problem.
We all found out last night.

The pants and shirt are WAY too big.
Can't the grown-ups get it right?

I guess when you are five years old.
It's never going to fit.

And Derek Jeter wouldn't care
When it comes his turn to hit.

Rally Caps

Did you ever wear a rally cap?
Do you think it really works?

It gets everybody excited
Tho' some say we all look like jerks.

You put your hat on backwards
And wear it inside out.

Then stand up in the dugout
And begin to stomp and shout.

And if the leadoff man gets on
You stomp and shout some more

Good things are gonna happen soon
How many runs will score?

And when the inning's over
And you've all done the high five slap

You know the reason you scored six runs
Was because of the rally caps!

Striking Out

We all know what it means
For a player to strike out.

But did you ever stop to think
What his feelings are all about?

You either swing and miss
Or hear the umpire yell "Strike Three!"

Either way you feel bad
Right there for all to see.

It really happens quite a bit
Much more than you probably think.

And anyone can tell you that
It's a feeling that really stinks.

Next Level

I have a chance
To move up a notch
And finally play in majors.

Of course I know
That I'll suddenly be playing
With much, much better players.

If I stay where I am
I'll hit .300, play short
And rarely have to sit out.

Or I can move on up
And sit on the bench
And when I play I'll mostly strike out.

So I guess it's easy
Why would I move up?
I'm happy right here where I am.

So tell the coaches "No thanks"
I'll stay here in the minors
Where I'm happy as a clam.

Pressure

I wonder if other kids hear this.
Pressure from Mom and Dad.

"Finish your homework or you just won't play"
Is that fair? Why are they so mad?

They know how important the game is to me.
And the team will lose if I'm gone.

So why do they do this? It makes everyone mad.
What's really going on?

It's only fifth grade. What's the big deal
If I get an A, B or C?

Baseball is BASEBALL, it's what I love.
It's what's really important to me.

But I know I must do it . . . or I really won't play.
I know that I just have no choice.

I guess that they're right. But I still want to know.
Is it the same for the other boys?

Put Me In, Coach!

I'd sure like to pitch
Out there on the mound
I bet I could strike 'em all out!!!

But my coach says "No way!
We might lose the game!
And winning is what it's about."

His kid gets to pitch
(And play shortstop and first)
Each and every game.

I don't think it's fair
That I don't get a chance.
In fact, I think my coach is pretty lame.

Okay, yeah, I know
That I'm not the best
And that I may never be great.

But come on, coach, get real!
It's not the World Series!
In fact, we're all seven and eight!

November

The World Series is over
No more baseball on TV
What a sad, sad time
It is for me.

Four more months
'Til spring training is here
How can I last?
It's the worst time of year.

Football's okay and
Basketball's not bad
But my favorite's the one
With the ball and the bat.

Last year was the same
Now I remember
Why I feel depressed
Every November.

Gotta Have A Dog

I'll bet you can't go
To a major league game
And not have a hot dog to eat.

With mustard and relish
And onions and ketchup
The messier the better—what a treat!

Let's Buy It!

I need a new bat
So shopping we go.
To the sporting goods store.
The best one we know.

I try 'em all out
With a great, mighty swing.
Dad yells out—
"Just don't hit anything!"

"I'll take this one", I say.
"No this one, no THIS!"
I'll get a hit each time.
I'll never, never miss.

Dad says, "Which one"
You have to decide.
I think that's the 23rd
Bat that you've tried!"

I say, "This is it!
It's the one that I choose.
By the way, can I also
Get a new pair of shoes?

2002

Nothing could be better
Nothing else would do
Like being an Angels fan in 2002!

Grandma

My grandma will come
To watch me play.
Not all the time
Just on hot, sunny days.

She doesn't know baseball
Doesn't care if we won.
And always asks me if I
Scored a home run.

I tell her, "But Granny
You HIT a home run
And she smiles and says
"Dear, as long as it's fun."

Breakin' It In

You just can't use a
New glove in a game.
It's just not usable
The way that it came.

It's much, much too stiff
And takes special care
Before it is ready
To take it out there.

Break it in first
'Til it's not loose and not tight.
Get it to where
It feels just right.

NOW you can use it
It was sure worth the wait.
Does it feel good now?
No . . . it feels super great!

Which?

I don't know
If this has happened to you
But I sure was embarrassed.
What should I do?

My turn to bat
Was coming up soon.
But I really REALLY
Had . . . to use the bathroom!

More 2002

Did I mention that first off
We knocked off the Yanks?
When nobody, NOBODY
Gave us a chance.

Next for the pennant
We matched up with the Twins.
We were off to the World Series
After four more big wins.

In the Series we faced
Mr. Bonds and his crew.
Let the championship parade begin!
I loved 2002!

Then

Look at the boys in the Little League Minors!
They're so amazingly small!

Look at them! Just look at them!
They're only three feet tall!

I know, when we were just their age
On this very same field here.

We couldn't have been that small, could we?
And when was that? Last year!